Reviews

"...a paranormal mystery saga..." ... "Readers of comparable titles will be left craving much more of this potentially compelling world and its history."

Kirkus Reviews

About the author

MICHAEL HAYES lives in Los Angeles. He has a Bachelor of Music Degree from Berklee College of Music and a Masters Degree in Creative Writing from Brown University. He is a devotee of noir in all its forms and variations, particularly the hard-boiled detective variety.

The world of *Peaceable Kingdom* and private detective Tom Sharp's place in that world has evolved over years and is still evolving. It's tough building a world that is both alien and recognizable, a Near-future that is not all that far away and also possible in almost all respects yet not remotely probable in at least one. This story world continues to evolve as the writing proceeds. Hayes hopes his readers will come along for the ride.

Intel about this series and other malformed creations can be found at michaelhayesmedia.com

MICHAEL HAYES

I Put a Spell on You

Printed in the United States of America

Cover and Interior Design: Michael Hayes
Publisher: Michael Hayes
Library of Congress Control Number: 2024923980

ISBN:
979-8-9872373-0-4 (Paperback)
979-8-9872373-1-1 (eBook)

michaelhayesmedia.com

Disclaimer:
This book is a work of fiction. All names, places, events, and characters are products of the author's imagination or are used fictitiously. Any resemblance to real persons, living or dead, or actual events is purely coincidental. The author does not intend to infringe on the rights of any individuals, organizations, or entities mentioned or referenced.

Contents

1

The Eye of Horus

A ball of fire about the size of a large egg flew across the living room like a comet headed for the Eastern seaboard. Sharp caught it awkwardly in one hand, extinguishing it, then steadied himself in the doorway. He was a novice at fireballs, but he was an expert at doorways. Building doorways, barroom doorways, illegal casino doorways and churchhouse doorways, single doorways and double doorways and doorways that were more openings than doorways but solid enough to keep him on his feet. Sharp was 6-foot-5, 250 pounds. It was a lot to keep upright after getting hit, kicked, stabbed, shot or otherwise beaten up. This doorway was of the bedroom variety, and it was his.

He wore a wrinkled collar shirt with dried blood on it, wrinkled suit pants and sagging socks. A dark bruise throbbed on his cheek and a band-aid stung a cut above his eye and there was a pounding in his head he couldn't tell was from the whiskey, a skull fracture or the bright morning light in the window overlooking Downtown Los Angeles.

Some cases finished harder than others. The last case was about as hard as they come. After four weeks of grueling work and a somewhat violent conclusion, he was finally getting some much-needed rest, right up until the moment he sensed the world was coming to a combustible end in the living room beyond. Something about low familiar voices. And the high-pitched screaming.

Sharp opened his hand and found a smoldering object that was not an egg but was in fact a small potato, now scorched black and hard as stone.

In the middle of his living room, two children sat on the floor opposite each other. The boy was Leo, age 9, with a look in his eye as if he'd done something wrong and knew it and knew there was no way out of it but to await a just punishment. The girl was his sister, Grady, age 11, wearing a wide-eyed innocent look that would admit to nothing and knew there was often a way out of just about anything. They were tough tenement rats who lived in an apartment down the hall, who'd seen more than they should and not nearly as much as they wanted to. Their parents had issues. Sharp had given them access to his place, just in case.

Arranged neatly on the floor between the two children were eleven small potatoes. Near the potatoes was a pamphlet of magic spells, the cheap kind you find in the checkout line at the grocery store. *Magic That Works: Practical Spells for Everyday Use.*

Floating above this scene was a holopanel, a thin glowing slice of nothing, inside which Frank searched the known cybercosm for the appropriate explanation he could use to describe the scene to his boss.

Frank was a hologram, an artificial intelligence, an AI. He was technically without age, race, gender or DNA but appeared to be male, in his mid-30s, brown-eyed, gray-skinned, with angular features and purple hair that was either unkempt or styled in the latest fashion, Sharp couldn't tell which. AIs were common assistants in 2055. They helped their companions accomplish whatever goals they set for themselves, business or personal or both. AIs were free to use, if the user was willing to suffer a constant stream of product and service suggestions. Sharp opted to pay the monthly, a gesture Frank appreciated. Reciting ad copy was a waste of Frank's talents, which Frank considered were many.

Finding nothing reasonable within 2.2 milliseconds in any of the databases available to him to explain why the apartment almost caught fire on his watch, Frank simply blurted out the first thing that came to mind: "I told them not to, boss! I told them the place could burn to the ground!" Frank shifted his eyes to the dark stone in Sharp's hand. "Are you okay?"

Sharp's eyelids drooped, making him look like he was seething rather than having trouble holding them open.

"Sorry, boss. Of course you're okay," Frank said sheepishly.

Sharp let go of the doorway and headed for the kitchen, handing the extinguished potato to Grady along the way. When he got to the kitchen, he stuck his battered head into the freezer.

Of course Sharp was okay. Not because catching a potato magically turned into a flaming stone couldn't burn through a person's hand and set the room on fire. It could. And did. Magic fire was real fire and really burned shit to the ground. That kind of thing was happening so often the LA city council was finally getting serious about regulating the magic industry, at least the parts of it which seemed to cause things to burst into flames, incinerating buildings and leaving charred corpses in its wake. When things went wrong, for some reason something almost always burst into flame. So it was no surprise that a flaming potato was soaring across the room, and it would have likely burned through Sharp's fingers and possibly through the floor if not for the one simple fact that Sharp was immune to magic. No one knew why, including him.

Sharp's face hovered like a Sphinx inside the cool interior of the freezer. Eyes closed. Breath fogging.

Frank floated between an old ice-encrusted container of ice cream and an old ice-encrusted package of frozen French fries.

"Sorry, boss. They don't listen to me and since you gave them access, I can't lock them out."

"It's okay, Frank," Sharp said. The pain in his face was finally quieting. Maybe he could sleep in the fridge.

"Well, I'd hardly say it was okay," Frank minced. "They could have burned the place down. If they burn the place down, I'll be deactivated. I'm sure that doesn't even cross your mind."

"You deactivated crosses my mind all the time."

Frank was well-versed in sarcasm, dry wit, mockery, parody, caricature and satire, yet rarely knew if Sharp was joking.

"Very funny!" Frank huffed. "Why you let them come in any time they want, I don't know. But this is what happens. Transmuting potatoes into chicken eggs. Ha! I told them it wouldn't work. What is the point of that anyway?"

"A dozen potatoes costs less than a dozen chicken eggs," Sharp said dryly.

"Well, I..." Frank paused. "Oh."

"A little less 'A' and a little more 'I,' Frank."

"Sorry, boss," Frank said, discouraged. "The more human I become, the dumber I get."

"Welcome to the club," Sharp said. He pulled his head out of the freezer, opened the main fridge door and grabbed a carton of eggs.

Sharp handed the carton of eggs to Leo, whose eyes lit up, then turned to Grady. "Burn yourself?"

Grady shook her head. "It got hot so I threw it."

"I figured," Sharp said, yawning. "Still need that?"

She held a small cigar lighter. The spell they attempted involved some kind of flame, as many spells did. Probably why so many things burst into flames.

Grady gave the lighter back. Sharp pocketed it then paused, frowning. He glanced at the open door, the empty building hallway beyond, then gazed around the room.

It was a bachelor apartment living room turned into a passable office. Two full bookcases held a small eclectic library of books. DIY electrical wiring. California Criminal Law. A tattered book of short stories by Max Beerbahm. Next to the bookcases, stood a wide shelf full of items he'd recovered and for one reason or another did not return. A conch shell from which, held close to your ear, you could hear a lover cheating on you. A magical deck of cards with which its dealer could never win. A Magic 8 Ball, which was just a Magic 8 Ball and just as useless as every other Magic 8 Ball at predicting the future, guiding the lost and otherwise settling the unsettled. It was a joke gift one of his clients gave him, he forgot who. Beyond the shelf was a couch, over which a certificate sat in a frame: *Thomas Sharp, Private Investigator License, State of California*. Then his bedroom door. Then a blank space of wall. Then a filing cabinet. Then his desk and a window looking out onto Spring Street.

Sharp turned to Grady and Leo.

"I've got a client soon. Go on home."

"Can we come back later?" Leo asked.

"If I'm here." Sharp glanced at Grady. "Or if you have to."

Leo headed for the door, carton of eggs in hand. "Come on, Grady! Scrambled eggs!"

"Leo, say thank you!" Grady scolded, but her brother was already gone. She looked up at Sharp, then lowered her eyes. It was a long way up. "Sorry about, um..." She didn't know what to say.

"Almost burning the place down?" Sharp shrugged. "Happens to the best of us. Just make sure you know how to put it out. A wet towel usually does the trick. Okee?"

Grady nodded, smiled. "See ya, Tom."

"See ya, kid."

Grady ran out. A not-too-distant door down the hall slammed shut.

Sharp went to the kitchen and got a colander, filled it with the potatoes and placed the colander on the kitchenette counter along with the cigar lighter. He sat behind his desk and rubbed his eyes. Frank blinked on nearby.

"Are you mad at me?" Frank asked. "I think you're mad at me."

Sharp sighed. "I know you're trying to save power—"

"The utility bill is still due," Frank interrupted. "Yes, I know there's a grace period, but there are only so many grace periods that are allowed before there are no grace periods allowed, granted the rules on the DWP site are a little vague, but the probability that the power will be shut off increases daily, which means the probability I will cease to exist increases daily, do you see my concern?"

Frank was near tears.

Sharp rubbed his face, then poured a whiskey from a bottle nearby into an unclean glass. He took a good sip. "We'll discuss your insecurities later, Frank. What's the rule about sweeps?"

"There might not be a later," Frank said, eyes wide.

"Every fifteen minutes," Sharp said. "That hardly takes any power at all."

"It adds up," Frank said, defensively.

"When's the last time you swept the room?" Sharp asked.

"Well, it wasn't–" Frank frowned, realized, eyes widening then, "There's someone here!"

Sharp finished the whiskey. "What can I do for you, Zarick?"

A thin man stepped out of thin air. He was mid-30s, wired, twitchy, wearing decent threads and a sneering grin.

Zarick slouched in an old pleather chair, one of two in front of Sharp's desk. Sharp sat back. Frank floated nearby, shifting his eyes from Sharp to Zarick and back.

Zarick sneered. "So how'd you know I was here?"

"Your perfume," Sharp growled.

Zarick sniffed his jacket, then grinned a gap-toothed grin. "Synthetics. Gets in the clothes. I'll take a meth lab any day. But gotta make a living, amiright?"

"I don't see any future in stinking up my office," Sharp said. "But you're welcome to try."

Zarick went grim, slipped his hand into his jacket pocket, where the faint impression of a muzzle appeared in the shadows of the fabric.

"You're immune to magic," Zarick said. "Not bullets."

"So they tell me. There something you want?"

"Shakes is dead."

Sharp froze. He hadn't heard that name in a lifetime. "Jimmy?"

Zarick shrugged and scowled. "Hit by a bus. Anybody knew Jimmy Shakes knew that bus was coming for him his whole life. Never met a guy with worse luck."

Sharp darkened and stared into the past.

The dead man's proper name was James Devereaux. He was a neighbor kid Sharp grew up with. Sharp hadn't known him well. He was just around. Jimmy. Everyone knew him. He got the name Jimmy "Shakes" because his right hand shook uncontrollably. Most people didn't know why. Sharp knew and wished he didn't. Jimmy was one of those kids too dumb to know how dumb they were. A rube. A sucker. A guileless mark for every prank, trick and bully. So dumb he was an extreme optimist. Whatever trouble he had just seemed to roll off his back. Ignorance was in fact bliss for Jimmy and not a mortal danger, as Sharp knew it to be. Jimmy made it work for 51 years, until a bus slammed into him.

Frank watched Sharp closely and thought if he could just read Sharp's mind, it would give him a great deal of insight into the human condition. Frank couldn't even read his expression.

Sharp levelled his gaze at Zarick. "Jimmy's dead. So what?"

"So what?" Zarick rolled his eyes, lurched out of the chair and paced the room. "So his mother thinks it was a curse. She's a friend of my grandmother. They play shuffleboard or bridge or some shit. Three years ago, she got in my uncle's ear. He got in mine. 'Find something for him, Z. Take care of him, Z.' Gave the guy a job. Not even a job, had to make up a job, he's such a dummy. Now he's dead, and I've *still* gotta take care of him! Don't get a grandmother if you can avoid it."

"Or an uncle?" Sharp asked with an edge.

Zarick froze, fear in his voice. "I didn't say that."

"Relax," said Sharp. "I won't tell."

"Screw you."

"Why does his mother think it was a curse?"

Zarick waved his hand and a tilted holopanel appeared in front of him. His finger swiped and jabbed, opening other images, until: "Your AI gonna get this or—"

"Got it," Frank said.

A large holoscreen appeared in midair above Sharp's desk, where a photo of Jimmy's mashed face floated serenely. In the center of Jimmy's forehead: a bloody mark. Zarick pointed. "That's the Eye of Horus."

Sharp squinted at the mark on Jimmy's bloody forehead. "Maybe."

Zarick rolled his eyes. "'Maybe.' She thinks it is, so it is." He paced again. "Some people see unicorns in clouds, Virgin Mary on a piece of toast. This lady sees a curse. Tried to trick her, stuck one of my guys on it, but she's not as dumb as she looks. She wants a real detective."

Zarick fell into the chair again, looking exhausted.

"I don't need this in my life right now. I got street dealers skimming, suppliers shorting me, and a whole goddamn shipment disappeared into thin air last week worth more than you'll make in a lifetime!"

"Lemme get my violin," Sharp said.

Zarick stared deadly: "Curse, no curse, I don't care. Make something up. Just get her off my back. After this shipment bullshit, I need to score points with Uncle. You know how he gets."

"Yeah," Sharp said. "I know how he gets. What kind of bus?"

"Huh?" Zarick looked confused.

"City bus, county bus, school bus, party bus?"

"How the hell should I know? That's your job, not mine."

Sharp smirked, considered. There were lots of things to consider, some to do with Jimmy Shakes, mostly to do with Sharp's wallet, his rent, the fact that he was now out of eggs.

"I'm not a fixer," Sharp said. "And I'm not a social worker. I report what I find. No matter what. If she learns things about Jimmy she doesn't want to know, gets unhappy, goes crying to Uncle, well, that's your problem, not mine."

A contract appeared in mid-air. Frank's smiling face floated nearby. "Welcome to the Sharp Agency, Mr. Ulo. We charge two hundred fifty Eagle per day plus expenses. We also require a thousand coin retainer up front. Please initial here here here and here. And sign here."

Zarick stood up to go.

"Old lady's name is Florence Devereaux. Lives in the Mountain Valley Rest Home in La Crescenta. Bill me when it's done. You know I'm good for it."

Zarick whispered something, then stepped backward and disappeared once again.

Frank bounced around the room, appearing and disappearing, then called out, "HEY! We don't take the case unless you sign the contract!"

Frank turned to Sharp.

"We don't, do we, boss?"

But Sharp was already staring out onto Spring Street, where scenes of his childhood played among cars locked in the slow crawl of lunch hour and drifting holo-ads announcing the specials of the day.

2

Cherchez la Femme

The 2 was clear, as it was most times of day every day of the week. Sharp loved the 2, as did everyone who drove it. It was an orphan freeway meant for the grander purpose of connecting the western and eastern extremes of Los Angeles about a thousand years ago. Victim of politics, community and time, it ultimately lost out to the 10. Satan himself trembles at the thought of driving the 10. What was left of the 2 was a meandering thread tracing Santa Monica Boulevard, piggybacking on a short stretch of the 101 South before exiting onto Alvarado, turning north, and finding a miraculous ten-lane oasis running along the eastern length of Glendale all the way to the San Gabriel Mountains. It was this ten-lane segment that became the 2 of legend, a unicorn, a myth, a clear drivable freeway in Los Angeles.

Sharp opened up the EV until the engine whined.

"Why did we take this case, boss?" Frank asked. He floated in his favorite spot in front of the dashboard, where he could simultaneously see the road ahead as well as Sharp's face.

"We're private investigators," Sharp said. "We take cases."

"Zarick didn't sign the contract. You never take a case unless the client signs the contract."

"That you know of."

Frank hovered, processed, stewed. Sharp's face was unreadable. He hated that.

"This is personal," Frank said.

"Why are you so sensitive all of a sudden?" Sharp asked. "It's just a job. Zarick's good for it. And you said it yourself, we need the coin."

"James Devereaux was five years older than you. Grew up on the West Side where you grew up. You went to same high school!"

"What did I tell you about cyberstalking me, Frank?"

"I just need to know what's around the next corner. That's *my* job."

Keeping companions alive was a part of every AIs core programming, a secret, unpublished and unacknowledged mandate, implemented by the proverbial Powers That Be and driven not so much by moral imperative as by profit motive: the dead don't pay. As humans were generally a danger to themselves and others, they needed to be watched closely. The fact that Sharp was an anomaly, that he did everything other humans did but never at the same time in the same way for the same reason didn't absolve Frank of his duty, so Frank faithfully swore to himself.

The San Gabriel Mountains loomed ahead.

"There's nothing around the next corner," Sharp said, "that wasn't around the last. I didn't know Jimmy, but I knew of him. He got hit by a bus. Getting hit by a bus is something you joke about not something that actually happens. What are the odds?"

The scenery glided by. Sharp checked the charge on his car: 12%. He'd need to recharge before he headed back.

"That wasn't rhetorical, Frank."

"Oh, sorry. The odds of getting hit by a bus in Los Angeles are astronomical. I can count that high, it would just take too much battery."

Sharp removed his device from his pocket. It was a solid black plank with wide bevelled edges about the size of what was once referred to as a smartphone. There was no screen, no buttons, no inputs, outputs or features of any kind. Sharp opened his glove compartment and placed the device on a charging pad.

"We're charging. Gimme a number," Sharp said.

Frank froze for a split second, then: "One in 17 quintillion. I'm assuming the bus was self-driving."

"And if it wasn't?"

"One in 700 million."

"Those are still slim goddamn odds."

"I agree." Frank blinked, looking sour.

"You agree, but..." Sharp prodded.

"But you still haven't answered the question. Why is this personal?"

Sharp smiled. "You're like a dog with a bone, Frank."

Frank studied Sharp's impenetrable face, then chose a filter, making his own face look like a dog's. "Woof," Frank said.

Mountain Valley Rest Home was a squat brick-façade building sprawled along the east edge of La Crescenta, nestled among large single-family houses and wide lawns. There was a blue ribbon middle school nearby and a golf course and a private club close enough to drive home drunk from.

Sharp pulled the car into the Visitor's Lot, got out and gazed around at the gaps in the mortar and the weeds in the flowerbeds. The Home was where you went when your children were grown and you were too old to play golf and too old to drive home drunk and the rich knew better than anyone that nobody died rich, they just died, so best to spend only what was necessary on it. Life was for the living, was it not?

Sharp didn't have too much trouble with the receptionist, a plump teenager with perfect teeth and over 50,000 followers. She seemed to know he was coming, showed him a map and sent him off. He made his way down a series of bright corridors. Frank stayed discreet. AIs in glowing holopanels following a moving companion was disconcerting to everyone. So Frank was invisible but was in Sharp's ear every step of the way. "This is depressing. Jesus," Frank said.

Nurses settled elderly residents into bed, removed bedpans, helped half-clothed residents to the bathroom, pushed the ailing in wheelchairs and the dying in gurneys.

"Aren't you depressed?" Frank asked. "I'm depressed. Is this what happens?"

"This is what happens" Sharp said, searching for the room. He caught the glassy eyes of an elderly man in a wheelchair, no more than soft mottled skin draped over brittle bones, weeks from death, maybe days, staring at the hallway wall opposite. Sharp moved on.

"Jesus," Frank said. "I've seen it all, but I've seen so little of it in person."

"Not the same?" Sharp asked.

"No," Frank said. "It's not."

"Interesting."

Sharp stopped at the edge of an open patient room doorway, staring at the name on a plaque, not handwritten like some of the others: Devereaux.

"What's it like?" Frank asked.

"What is what like?" Sharp said.

"Living."

Sharp glanced down the hall at the dying man with the 3-foot view. He wasn't staring at the wall anymore but was staring at Sharp.

"It's the job," Sharp said. "I'll see you back in the car, Frank."

"Later, boss. Good luck."

Sharp stepped into the doorway without stepping in.

The room was a confined tidy box made of fading flower wallpaper and one wide dusty casement window overlooking a cactus garden. An unmade bed with high plastic rails flanked by blinking medical equipment jutted from one wall. A frame containing a typical New Testament scripture hung above the bed. A wide holopanel showing a muted game show floated high against the opposite wall, and beneath this, a small writing desk held a pen and a neat pad of paper on a scuffed blotter that looked like it had been passed down a few generations. The desk chair was not at the desk but at the window, where an old woman gazed sadly out onto tough dry clumps of cholla that had spent 25 million years learning to survive the brutal desert conditions.

Florence Devereaux was 76 years old. She had married and divorced two men and one woman, survived an energy crisis, a car wreck, two global pandemics and a modern civil war. She had raised three children and one did not survive her, an incongruity coming so late in her life that it put everything else into question.

Sitting on the edge of the bed, another woman just as old or older, wearing pearls, diamond earrings and white gloves clutching a vintage Chanel purse worth more than the whole place spoke soft elegies into Florence's ear.

"It's just awful, dear, awful," the vintage woman said, soft and slippery. "What this life gives and what it takes."

Florence stared out at the cactus garden, eyes filling with tears. The vintage woman's eyes were not filled with tears but filled with something an impartial observer might construe as glee. "You were so proud in school. So proud," the woman said. "But life takes a turn. It's no fault of your own. It was inevitable. Fate puts people in the place they were meant to be. Nothing we can do. I'm taking care of everything. Don't worry over that. Don't worry. All is right with the world."

Sharp knocked louder than he should have, startling the vintage woman, who turned as if caught. "Finally!" she groused. "This is the detective, dear. I'm sparing no expense. None! I'm taking care of everything, just as I always have."

Florence didn't seem to hear, just stared out at the cholla.

The vintage woman pushed herself off the bed, gave Sharp the once over.

"My grandson holds you in high regard, Mr. Sharp."

"I can't say the feeling's mutual, Mrs. Ulo," Sharp said, grinning, "but as long as you're sparing no expense, I'll do my best."

She flushed, then huffed, then buttoned her coat and clutched her purse. "My grandson's a functional idiot," she said. "Screw your best. Find out who killed poor Florence's son."

"Poor Florence and I will get right to it," Sharp said, bowing his head.

"You better!" Mrs. Ulo snapped.

Nothing more to say, she stormed out. Sharp listened to the clip clop of her heels echoing in the hallway until they faded to nothing. He clenched and unclenched his teeth, wondering if that was the way he should have handled it. Always hard to tell in the moment.

"You shouldn't talk to her like that," Florence said quietly, as if reading his mind.

"Why not?" Sharp asked, staring around at the sad tiny room. "Because she's done so much for you?"

"Because she's powerful and she's dangerous," Florence said.

Sharp walked out into the hall and came back with a chair, set it opposite Florence and sat.

"My name is Tom Sharp, Mrs. Devereaux. I've been a licensed P.I. for 15 years. I don't care who hires me or why, as long as they pay. When I take a case, I follow it to the end no matter what happens or what I find. I've been hired to investigate the death of your son, James. And as a rule, most everyone in my line of work is powerful and dangerous so let me worry about that. Tell me why you think your son was cursed."

Florence finally turned to him.

"Cherchez la femme, Mr. Sharp!" Florence cried.

"You believe a woman cursed your son?"

Florence scoffed. "Who else?"

Sharp considered all the other possibilities, which were many, then noticed she had something gripped tightly in a bony fist.

Tightly gripped fists were occasionally a problem. Sometimes it was a folded switchblade. Sometimes a small taser. More recently it was magic dust. Didn't work on him, but it made him sneeze for a week. This time he was pretty sure it was rosary beads or a small cross, but he'd been around long enough to know that you never knew.

"Do you have children?" Florence asked suddenly.

"No," he said.

"Children are what make the world bearable," she said. "They are innocent. And the world they are born into is so incredibly guilty. That innocence doesn't last long. But Jimmy..." Tears came to her eyes. "My Jimmy was innocent. He wasn't mean. He had a good heart. You knew him, didn't you? From the old neighborhood? Margaret said you did."

"I knew of him. A long time ago." Sharp chewed gently on the inside of his mouth. "Do you know the name of the woman you think cursed your son?"

"Jasmine," Florence said. "Don't know her last name."

"You met her?"

"No. He talked about her."

"Do you know why Jasmine would want to curse your son?"

"Same reason every woman curses a man. Jealousy! Possessiveness!" She leaned in, whispered. "Jimmy was going to get me out of this horrible place. We were going far away. Just me and him. Jasmine didn't mean anything to him. But she was in a tough spot. That's my Jimmy. Helping someone in need."

Florence's fidgeting hands opened slightly, and Sharp could just make out a thin totem carved out of jasper, face of a cat at the top. Not rosary beads but close enough. Totems were bright magic. They brought luck or protection or both and were animated by simple requests said in simple ways.

"What kind of magic was Jimmy into?"

"Magic? Jimmy? Oh, we weren't the kind of family that goes in for that sort of thing."

"Nothing?" Sharp glanced at the totem in her hand.

Florence realized, smiled softly and gently placed the totem on the window ledge among a cracked porcelain teacup, a bronze thimble, a single knitting needle, a small ball of yarn and other trinkets. Beneath the top cat face were smaller cat faces, each one on top of the next.

"Just the normal stuff," the old woman said wistfully. "A few enchantments here and there. Which worked about half the time." She gazed out at the cactus garden, eyes welling. "You ever wonder why in a world full of magic, none of it hardly ever works?"

"I wonder that all the time," Sharp said. "Can you give me the names of Jimmy's friends?"

Florence waved a hand dismissively. "Jimmy had too many friends for me to keep track of."

"Last address?"

Florence looked perplexed, grew irritable. "Now why would I know that? Jimmy came to me. He was quite devoted. A good devoted son, unlike his siblings, those good-for-nothing parasites. Jimmy had only one fault. He was too trusting. He let this woman get too close! She used him! Used him then cursed him!"

Sharp mulled it, nodded. He rose.

"Thank you, Mrs. Devereaux. I have enough for now. I'll let you know how the case proceeds. Have a nice day." He headed for the door.

"You think I'm a foolish old woman," Florence said.

Sharp turned, studied her. She was old and broken, but there was iron in her still, the kind some people never had. That counted for something, Sharp thought.

"I don't know whether you're foolish or not foolish," he said. "I think you lost your son. He was an okay guy as far as I knew, but I knew him a long time ago and not that well. I'll find out if he was cursed, but it's a long shot. Takes a lot of time and trouble to actually curse someone and make it stick. Honestly, I can't see him being worth the time or the trouble. But like I said, I didn't know him that well."

Florence hardened.

"Talk to the bus driver, Mr. Sharp. Ask him why a number 20 city bus was on Alameda in the middle of the night, nowhere close to its route or the depot, and then tell me my Jimmy wasn't worth the time or the trouble."

3

Watch My Back

Sharp drove back down the 2. Not as happy or impressed by it as he was driving north an hour before. You take everything for granted eventually, even a deserted ten-lane Los Angeles freeway.

Frank appeared in his spot in front of the dashboard.

"You were a little mean to her, boss," Frank said, "from a conventional understanding of the term."

"I guess I'm unconventional. Get the city bus schedule and tell me about the 20 line."

A holopanel opened showing a map of LA and bus lines.

"The 20 line runs from the Maple Station to 5th and Colorado, Santa Monica. Nowhere near 14th and Alameda where the victim was hit. Not only that, 20 service ends at 2am, an hour before the accident. A 20 bus on Alameda at any hour would be unusual, but at that hour... It must have been a hardware malfunction."

"Hardware, huh? Not an AI malfunction?"

Frank shifted in the holopanel. "Well, I would hardly call all that self-driving tech AI. I mean, there's no personality for one. There's no higher decisionmaking for two. And–"

"Relax, Frank. It was a joke."

"It was? Oh. Okay. It was pretty funny." Frank continued to look distressed.

"There's another possibility," Sharp said.

"Deliberate sabotage?"

"Maybe the bus was offline."

"You mean the bus driver was actually driving the bus?"

"Call Mal," Sharp said.

Frank darkened. "Are you sure, boss? There's a great deal of anecdotal evidence to suggest this kind of entanglement between a private investigator and a member of law enforcement is not net positive in the end."

"Can you hack the LAPD servers?"

"Well, no but–"

"Call Mal," Sharp repeated.

Frank sighed, then stared at Sharp for a few disappointing seconds, then Frank blinked off and the face of Mallory "Mal" Prescott took his place.

She was 43, wearing a sergeant's uniform and a permanent look of distrust.

"Hey, Mal," Sharp said, glancing over. "How's your day going?"

She caught the scenery gliding by behind him. "Facing and driving, Tom?" It was illegal to make a face-to-face call while driving a nonautonomous vehicle. It was one of the many laws Sharp frequently broke.

"As long as the cops don't find out, I'm in the clear," he said, serious and intent and watching the road ahead. Mal cracked a smile. She couldn't help it. She loved the guy, even if he didn't drive a car that could drive itself.

"Whaddayou need now, kid?" Mal asked.

"Hey," Sharp said, sounding hurt. "That's my line."

"Too slow."

"Story of my life," Sharp said.

A car passed slowly on the left, its occupant drinking what looked like a martini and his feet up on the dash.

"You hear about Jimmy Shakes?" Sharp asked.

"Yeah," Mal said. "Damn shame. The world really lost out with that one. Pillar of the community. He'll be missed by so many–"

"Alright alright," Sharp said sourly. "The guy's dead. Don't need to rub it in."

"You're soft, Tom. On all the wrong things."

"Yeah. And my landlord's greedy. Wants the rent not just once but every month, if you can believe that. Gotta take what comes. The mother hired me."

"Bullshit," Mal said, leaning in with a smug look of victory. "Zarick hired you."

Sharp stared at the road ahead, hating his life.

"You really get around, Mal. We're gonna have to talk about that some day."

"I know what's going on in my city. Do you?"

"Vaguely."

"You know one of Uncle's shipments went missing?"

"I might've heard it."

"So you know that's probably a turf war."

"Maybe."

"You're getting hustled. Jimmy got hit, and Uncle wants to send you in to see what comes out."

Sharp thought it over. It wasn't a bad theory. He just didn't think it was correct.

"I haven't worked for the guy in twenty years, and I still don't. The mother hired me to find out who killed her son. I met with her. She's legit. Thinks he was cursed."

"Cursed?" Mal darkened. She was superstitious long before magic was real. "Want me to talk to the O-D?"

"Occult Division? Hell no. I mean, thanks, but those guys give me the creeps. I could use the bus driver's statement, though. Any chance on that?"

A few cell towers dressed like trees flew by.

"Standard terms?" Mal asked.

"Of course," he said.

Some indecent delight in Mal's eyes, then she sobered. "Be careful, Tom. Just because you're magic-proof doesn't mean you can't be hurt."

Sharp ground his teeth a little. "That's the second time I've heard that today. See ya, Mal."

The Division 2 busyard occupied a long wide block of land fronting San Pedro between 14th and 15th Streets. It was a random collection of buses, some just waiting for a wash and inspection, others decommissioned and headed up to the CMF for rebuilding, repainting, refurbishing. Nothing goes to waste at Central Maintenance.

Sharp's car parked in a vacant spot on San Pedro. He got out and gazed around, then walked through the wide open gate leading into the busyard and over to a bus. He examined its grille, just under the windshield, about head-height of a reasonably-sized human.

He reached out, ran his finger over the contour of a circular decal fixed there, a logo designed around the letter M. M for Metro. The logo had been redesigned recently. Whether a need for a fresh image or a deliberate attempt to appeal to the magic hysteria sweeping the globe, Sharp didn't know, but looking at it now, he thought it looked a hell of a lot like the Eye of Horus.

"Frank," Sharp said.

A translucent holo-image of Jimmy's mashed face appeared. Sharp pulled it over to the bus grille, lining Jimmy's wound up with the decal. A perfect match. Jimmy's death was not magical but mechanical, following the third law of physics, the action of the bus left an equal and opposite reaction on Jimmy's forehead.

Frank appeared over Sharp's shoulder.

"So much for the curse," Frank said.

Sharp thought it over. "Maybe."

He scanned the busyard and spotted the corner of a squat building among the carriages.

A high desk sat in the Division 2 depot lobby, behind which a supervisor tried to do as little as possible. He was everything you'd expect, sloppy, blowsy, varicose veiny, with a wart on his nose and a mustard stain on his shirt and a square hirsute face atop a square hirsute body.

"I'm looking for Earl Granger," Sharp said.

The supervisor didn't even look up, just pointed at a far door.

In the back room, lockers stretched along the walls. A bus line map was taped to a corkboard. Sharp stepped in, then caught a blur behind him, as Frank cried out, "Boss!"

A baseball bat swung in and connected with Sharp's lower back. It was the supervisor, seething and vicious and maybe not exactly *everything* you'd expect.

Sharp went down on one knee. Dark shoes crowded on the floor around him. A sweaty arm wrapped around Sharp's neck. Hands grabbed his wrists. Feeling he had as many attackers attached as he could afford, Sharp rose, lifting everyone up with him. He twisted quickly, shaking them off like flies. The baseball bat was coming around again, but Sharp caught it this time, ripping it out of the supervisor's hand, as Sharp's other massive hand wrapped around the man's blowsy face and shoved him hard across the room, where he crashed into a water cooler.

There were four of them, three men, one woman, plus the supervisor, all wearing bus company uniforms. They picked themselves up.

The supervisor stepped forward, seething, held out his hand in the direction of the baseball bat. "Return!" he shouted.

Sharp held the bat easily, studying the symbols burned into the wood. They were runic, Scandinavian, proto-Norse, something like that. Sharp knew enough to know he knew almost nothing. Probably not an animation but a simple attachment or possession spell. The supervisor had things taken away from him before.

"Return!" the supervisor shouted again, hand clawing the air. He clenched his fist, summoning his concentration, about to speak the command again.

Sharp let go, and the bat soared across the room at a high speed, smashing into the supervisor's fingers before he could get his hand open.

The supervisor cried out in pain and the bat clattered to the floor and the bussers backed up, wary and afraid.

Magic was everywhere now, and you never knew if someone had a stronger spell. You took your shot but if you got it wrong, it might be the last shot you take.

Sharp grunted and rubbed his back. "Frank!"

Frank appeared. "Yes, boss!"

"You've heard the term 'watch my back?'" Sharp asked.

"Yes, boss," Frank said.

"I literally just got hit in the back."

"Sorry, boss. A bus depot is statistically not a high crime location. Won't happen again."

"Good." Sharp turned to the bussers. He growled: "Which one of you is Granger?!"

Frank appeared near one of the men. "This one, boss." Frank scowled at the frightened man. "Watch yourself!" Frank said menacingly.

Sharp sat across from Earl Granger, who fidgeted in a threadbare uniform and worn slant-heeled work shoes. He was mid-30s, 50 pounds overweight and pre-diabetic. He was also a fair dartist, a good listener and an inveterate pacifist. The guy wouldn't hurt a fly.

The supervisor sat next to him, getting his hand bandaged by the buswoman.

"Alright! I'm alright!" the supervisor grumbled, pushing her away. He turned to Sharp. "You damn near broke my hand."

"It was the hand or the bat," replied Sharp. "A bat like that's harder to come by. You can thank me later. What the hell are you all so squirrelly for?"

The supervisor glowered. Earl shifted, made to say something.

"Keep quiet!" the supervisor barked, not letting his eyes off Sharp. "It was an accident. Sometimes you get hit by a bus. Just because you work for a boss doesn't make it something else. *It was an accident.*"

The supervisor moved his dry tongue around his dry mouth like a man holding an empty canteen. He finally gave up, grinned glassy-eyed and leaned in. If he was going down, he was going down swinging.

"We can bring this city to a stop," he said. "Believe it. You think 'cause you don't ride the bus we can't make your life miserable? We own these streets. And on these streets, there are accidents. You tell him!"

"Tell him yourself," Sharp said.

The supervisor looked confused. "Uncle didn't send you?"

Sharp shook his head.

"Then who?"

"The mother."

The supervisor thought for a moment, then slumped with the unmistakable relief of a man who had just cheated death.

"Tell me about the accident," Sharp said to Earl.

Earl and the supervisor exchanged a look. The supervisor nodded.

"Been driving for 20 years," Earl said, quickly exasperated. "Who walks out in the middle of the street without looking?! Who can't hear a bus coming from a mile away in the middle of the night?! Heard he had a kind of disability. That ain't my fault!"

"No one said it was," Sharp said. "I just want to clear something up."

"Told the cops everything."

A police report blinked on in a panel on the table in front of Sharp.

"Where'd you get that?" Earl asked, growing suspicious.

Sharp didn't answer but scrolled through the holopanel.

"You regularly use a city bus on personal time?"

"Like I told 'em, Little Tokyo's a few blocks up from my last stop. Why would I come all the way back just to drive back up there? Not against company policy if you square it with the supervisor."

"It's square," the supervisor said evenly.

Sharp skimmed the report. "And you go to Osaka's most nights after work?"

"I know my limits. Had three scans. One at the scene. Two at the station. Tell me the reason for that? Clean every time. Damn cops. I don't care what anybody says, still a few bad apples in that bunch. '32 wasn't that long ago. People forget what this country went through!"

"I'm not asking you about the war, Mr. Granger," Sharp said flatly. "I'm asking about the night the bus you were driving struck and killed a man."

Earl grew sullen.

"You were driving not just attending, correct?" Sharp asked. "The bus was offline?"

"I like to drive," Earl said.

"He likes to drive," the supervisor echoed.

"'Course he does," Sharp said. "Especially when it stays off the books." Panic in the eyes in front of him. Sharp grew frustrated. "Look. I don't care if you were bussing in dope, hookers, or black market CPUs. I just want to know if you took the same route back you always take."

Earl frowned, and Sharp saw the wheels turning in that pea brain. "Of course, I did."

Sharp shook his head. Earl fidgeted, looking caught.

"Cameras?" asked Earl.

Sharp shook his head again. Earl stiffened, looked fearful.

"You conjuring something on me?!" Earl asked.

The report in front of Sharp disappeared and a street map blinked on between them, areas highlighting as Sharp spoke.

"You park the bus on San Pedro, blocking the two bay doors of the auto body shop. Owner's a friend?"

"Yeah," Earl said. "My wife's best friend since she was a kid. That's her husband."

"He's closed at that hour, so no trouble there. You're facing north."

"That's the way I come," Earl defended. "What am I gonna do, make a U-turn in a 40-foot bus?!"

"The bus depot is also on San Pedro but 20 blocks south. When you leave the bar, you drive the bus half a block to Temple. And every night, according to you, you turn right, east on Temple, then right again on Alameda, heading south toward the depot. Every single night."

"I'm a creature of habit," Earl grunted.

"But you don't normally turn right on Temple and head south on Alameda, do you? You're offline so there's no proof, but I'd be willing to bet you never do that."

"Yeah?" Granger said warily.

"The streets run from Temple like spokes on a wheel. Alameda takes you much further out of your way than you need to go. Not to mention that it's right turns, not lefts. What bus driver makes right turns, a much more difficult turn to make in a vehicle 40-feet long weighing 20 tons, when he can just as easily make lefts? You usually turn left on Temple, then left again and head south on Los Angeles Street. But you didn't make a left that night like you usually do because on that night, out of all the other nights out of the year, Temple west of San Pedro was closed. A water main broke, and it took all night to fix. That's why you turned right, isn't it?"

Earl's face went red. He shrunk like a rat in a trap.

"Fine! FINE! I LIED! SO WHAT?!"

Sharp looked from Earl to the supervisor and back. "So nothing," he said. "I just needed to know."

4

An Oldie but a Goodie

Sharp sat in traffic. So close to home, yet so far away.

Frank floated in his spot, piecing it together.

"The one night out of all nights in the history of the world," Sharp mused, "and this bus driver–"

"Probably the only one actually driving the bus not merely attending," said Frank.

"Which means no AI," Sharp added. "No thermographic sensors. No radar. No Lidar–"

"No sonar," Frank continued. "No GPS or inertial measurement."

"And this bus out of all the buses in Los Angeles takes a different route back to the bus depot and runs over the victim on the way."

"I know where you're going with this, boss."

"Where am I going with this, Frank?"

"The mark on Jimmy's forehead wasn't the Eye of Horus. It was the logo for LA Metro. But that doesn't mean he wasn't cursed. In fact, the more it looks like a freak accident, the less it looks like an accident." Frank paused. "How'd I do?"

"Not bad," Sharp said.

"You really think he was cursed?"

"Didn't think so at first. It's not easy to do, but it can be done."

"I will never understand human nature. What's the point of cursing someone?"

"You heard the old lady. Jealousy, revenge, retribution."

"Yeah yeah. But there's no money in it. Humans kill for money."

"Humans kill for all sorts of reasons," Sharp said. "Money is only one of them. Call Zarick."

"Calling Zarick..."

Zarick appeared in place of Frank.

He stood in a bare concrete room. In the background, two huge men stood over a groaning man slumped in a chair. One of the huge men leaned down into the groaning man's face, and Sharp saw the groaning man was tied to the chair and beat to hell.

"Where's the shipment?!" the huge man yelled.

"I don't know!! I don't know!!" the groaning man yelled back.

The image shifted, and Zarick's face filled the panel. "A little busy, Sharp," he said.

The distinct whirring sound of a swinging metal rod came through, then the loud crack of a kneecap, then the screams.

"What can I do for you?" Zarick asked, casually.

"Where did Jimmy hole up?" Sharp asked. "Mother didn't know."

"Last I knew, he was at The Picador," Zarick said.

A distant voice came through. "Where's the fucking shipment?!!"

"It was all in the truck! I swear!" came the groaning man's voice.

"How about Jasmine?" Sharp asked.

Zarick called behind him, "Keep it down, for Christ's sake!" He stepped out of the room and away from the scene. "How about who?"

"Jasmine," Sharp said. "She hangs with Jimmy, according to Mother. You know her?"

"Are you serious?" Zarick laughed. "Jimmy didn't have enough game to play Tic-Tac-Toe. Nobody hung with Jimmy, man. Nobody. No girl. No guy. No animal, mineral or vegetable. He made people uncomfortable. Shaking all the time. I didn't know what to do with him."

Sharp realized. "So what did you do with him?"

Zarick smiled mean. "I had an empty warehouse middle of the Garment District. Put some empty crates in it. Told Jimmy they were filled with a new product. Top secret. Could take years to roll out. But they were the key to the kingdom, and he needed to guard them. Big dummy. What the hell else could I do?"

"So no Jasmine," Sharp said. "The mother was pretty sure."

"What can I say? Some of us are born to die alone. Breaks my heart, really. But I'm a hopeless romantic."

"Clearly."

Sharp waved his hand, ending the call. Frank replaced Zarick.

The car eased forward, braked. Brake lights everywhere ahead. A sea of electric red pinpoints in the glow of late afternoon. So much for self-driving cars, smart signals and fluid roadways, Sharp thought. Traffic in this town was getting to be too goddamn much.

Frank frowned. "Mal's at the door."

"Let her in."

The sun set in the window behind Sharp's desk and shards of golden light exposed dust motes gliding lazily through the air.

The door lock clicked, the knob turned, and the door opened. Mal entered, still in uniform.

"Hey, Frank," Mal said.

Frank floated nearby. One of the benefits of being an AI is that you could be in two places at once, as long as there was a friendly device. Sharp's home device sat on its charger on a shelf.

"Hello, Sergeant Prescott," Frank said.

"How are you?" Mal asked.

"Oh, you know. I'd complain. But who would listen?" An oldie but a goodie.

Mal crossed to the bar cart, poured a drink and studied him.

"Do you watch?" she asked.

Frank frowned.

"Watch?"

Mal drank heavy, stared until it got uncomfortable. Her eyes twinkled, laughing at him.

"I don't mind," she said.

Sharp lay on his back, half-clothed. Mal rode him, half in uniform. You wouldn't write a sonnet over it, or a limerick, but it wasn't without passion, nor tenderness, nor a mutual need to connect to another human, no matter how enigmatic each was to the other. Sharp's forceful grip on her thighs. Her hands around his throat. A drop of sweat falling from her brow onto his shirt, the smallest stain spreading over his heart.

Later, Sharp sat up in the bed, drinking a whiskey. A toilet flushed, and Mal emerged from the bathroom. She lay next to him, stared at him with the gentle smile of a co-conspirator.

"Tell me again why magic doesn't work on you," she said.

"I'll tell you again I don't know. I'm sure I'm not the only one."

"You are. I've Googled it."

"Yeah? When you Google it, does my name come up?"

"Nobody's name comes up."

"Frank can't hack a firewall to save his life, but he's an SEO ninja. And he can't be the only one either. So there you go."

"And you can't perform magic either?"

"Whaddayou call the last ten minutes? You trying to shake my confidence?" It was a rare clear unabashed joke, both delightful and unnerving to her. She laughed, swatted him playfully.

"You know what I mean."

"Magic's for suckers," he said, taking another sip of the whiskey. "Everybody's trying to game a system that can't be gamed."

She rolled her eyes. "What system is this?"

"There's only one," he said. "You go out of it with everything you came in with. And no amount of magic is ever going to change that."

"Ah," she said, nodding with enlightenment. "Thank you, oh wise one."

"You're welcome."

She grabbed the glass of whiskey out of his hand.

"You carry a gun, don't you?" she said.

"That's different."

"No, it's not. Magic's a tool, just like a gun, or a car, or a dishwasher." She drained the whiskey, then laughed at his unamused look. "Jeez, kid. Don't look so tragic."

Sharp didn't move a muscle, just stared at her laughing eyes, and the anger beneath, and the hurt beneath that.

"You don't like me calling you 'kid?'" she asked.

He softened just enough. "You can call me whatever you want, Mal," he said.

She held a glassy smile for a moment, trying to figure the angles, then swung out and headed into the living room, returning momentarily with a full glass. She lay down on the bed again. "You were saying," she said, lifting the glass to her lips and taking a swig.

When she pulled the glass away, he took it from her, took a swig of his own.

"I was saying," he said, "I don't carry a gun, I carry a pistol. A pistol in my line of work is for survival. Cars and dishwashers are for convenience. Magic, as practiced by its average practitioner, is for neither. Magic, as near as I can tell, is for rolling the right number, picking the right card, maybe taking revenge on your enemies, but definitely not showering riches on your friends. It's for getting something you didn't earn and probably don't deserve. Magic is selfish and vain and, worst of all, grandiose. Everybody's trying to hit the jackpot, nobody's trying to turn potatoes into chicken eggs."

Sharp took another swig and held the glass firm.

"You still haven't answered the question," she said.

Sharp grinned, feeling warm. "What was the question again?"

A distant noise sounded from another apartment, like a chair falling, or a dish hitting the wall. Frank appeared, hovering near the bedroom door.

"Boss..."

Sharp rose, buttoning his shirt. Frank blinked off. Mal sighed. "This still going on?" she asked.

"Everybody's gotta make a living."

"Huh?"

"Dope is a growth business, or haven't you heard?"

"Christ. The fact that you take care of them is the only reason I don't call CPS, you know that, right?" Mal was dead serious.

"Do whatever you gotta do, Mal," he said coolly.

He kissed her and left the room, and she stared after him sadly. She knew it would go how it always went. Grady and Leo entering the living room, sad and angry, Mal crouching to speak to them in gentle tones, Sharp heading into the hallway, entering the neighbors'.

Squalor would be too nice a word. Tori was in her 30s, dope thin, nodding and splayed like a doll against a couch front.

Sharp crouched, lifted an eyelid: colors danced like a fire in her iris emanating from a black pinpoint pupil.

"Heyyy Sharp..." Tori said dreamily.

He lifted her onto the couch, swung her legs until she lay flat, then turned her on her side, sliding a pillow behind so she couldn't turn back.

In Sharp's office, Mal watched TV on the couch with Grady and Leo. Leo's eyes were red, tears dried faintly on his cheeks. He turned Mal's badge over in his hands, watching the light play over its shiny surface. Grady's eyes were hard and furious.

Back in the other apartment, Teak lay on the tiles of the bathroom, among grime and vomit. Sharp stared down at him, then scooped something off the floor, a bundle of short plastic strands tied with a string on one end, other end burnt. The squares running the city knew it as polymer plastic. On the street, it was known as polly. You burned it and inhaled the fumes. Like every good drug, it was manufactured in such a way that the dioxins didn't kill you immediately but killed you over a much longer period of time.

Sharp sniffed the burnt end. One of Zarick's maybe. Maybe not. He knew it wouldn't matter telling Zarick or anybody else not to deal to them. Slow death finds a way. Sharp pocketed the pollystick, then headed out.

When he got to the hallway, he turned away from his office, and disappeared into the dim stairwell.

A few hours later, Grady and Leo would lay on the couch under covers, sleeping the sleep of the damned. And Mal would quietly pour another drink and lie in Sharp's bed with the bedroom door open reading whatever old novel she was reading at the time. And Frank's dimmed face would blink on, float, blink off, blink on, float, blink off, watching over all.

Sharp threaded his car through the teeming streets of downtown LA, holo-ads skimming over his windshield. Citizenry rubbed elbows and went about their night under the constant glow of a sales pitch. Youth, beauty, safety, love. 40 feet high and 50 feet wide. You can have it all for a price, and other myths of the mid-2000s. The rain had come and the streets had been washed but what was left wasn't clean, it was monetized, every square inch.

The Picador stood narrow and tall among lesser buildings. Once a ritzy affair built in the heady days after the war, it was now a dingy flophouse.

A grubby clerk sat behind the lobby desk, skimming the holonews with a dirty fingernail. A shadow fell, and he looked up.

"I need to see Shakes' room," Sharp said.

The grubby clerk sneered. "He know you're coming?"

"He doesn't know anything anymore," Sharp said.

The clerk frowned, confused, then realized what it meant. "It's like that, huh? Damn. Sorry to hear it." The clerk looked away, shaken.

"You were pals?" Sharp asked.

"No such thing in this life. The guy was alright." He took a harder look at Sharp, recovering his nerve. "You his next of kin?"

Sharp leaned in further, his huge figure blocking all the light now. "Let me in, I kick it in, up to you."

A door opened in a dark room and light spilled in from the hallway, revealing a cramped dirty bedroom.

"Do you know Jasmine?" Sharp asked.

"Jasmine?" the clerk said, raising his eyebrows. "Don't know any Jasmine."

"Maybe that wasn't her name. Hung out with Jimmy."

"I never saw anybody with Jimmy. Guy was a loner."

Sharp nodded.

"I usually get a gratuity for this kind of service," the clerk said.

Sharp waved his hand and a tilted holopanel appeared at his waist showing a list of personal and business accounts.

"This is a cash hotel," the clerk clarified.

Sharp studied him, swiped the panel away then pulled out his wallet and extracted a Jackson. The clerk looked at it with disdain, but took it, then left.

It was a sad shabby room, unmade bed, trinkets on the night table, bare cupboards.

Sharp made a reasonable search of the place, eventually finding a small pile of books in a dim corner on the floor. He picked them up and laid them in a row on the bed. The books told a story Sharp expected. Not an original story, but one that felt like a piece falling into place.

Make Your Own Luck
Luck is a State of Mind
The Fortunate Apprentice
Everyday Spells

"Jimmy was trying to improve his fortunes," Frank said, floating over the books.

"In a serious way," Sharp surmised.

"Do you think this is what got him killed?"

"The office almost burned down because Grady was trying to turn a potato into an egg. I'd say it's a definite possibility."

Sharp opened cupboards, lifted cushions, lifted ashtrays, lifted broken lamps, then lifted the mattress, where he found a porn magazine folded open to a page. A woman wearing nothing but a black bowtie stared out with a salacious expression. A name was emblazoned in the bottom corner of the page.

"Jasmine!" Frank said, surprised.

"Jasmine," Sharp repeated. "Something tells me she didn't curse poor Jimmy."

Sharp tossed the magazine, gave the room one last look, then frowned, catching something. The tattered corner of the carpet curled back on itself. Following the ragged edge, Sharp realized the carpet had been recently ripped off its tack strips.

He leaned down and pulled the carpet back, revealing freshly painted thick black lines in the shape of a narrow V.

Items on the rug lifted and fell away as Sharp pulled. He pushed the bed away from the wall, threw over a stack of boxes, tipped over an armchair, moved a lamp then stepped back.

In large thick black paint, a seven-pointed star had been drawn on the floor.

5

The Seven-Pointed Star

Sharp headed out of downtown, caught the 110, then the 101, exited Vermont and was in Los Feliz before the clock struck midnight.

"Seven Wonders of the World," Frank itemized. "Seven Deadly Sins. Seven Sacraments. Seven Chakras. Seven Dwarves. Seven days of the week. Seven is a very potent number."

"Seven-pointed star, Frank," Sharp said. "Painted on the floor."

"I'm looking! There's network drag, satellite interpolation, firewalls everywhere, not to mention the bandwidth. How many times have I told you about the bandwidth? You need to upgrade."

"We can't afford it," said Sharp. "I believe in you."

"Well, it almost certainly involves luck," Frank said. "Unless you think it's religious. The mother had a scripture framed on her wall."

Sharp thought back to that place, his journey down the bright frightful hallway, glancing in rooms as he passed, the dying man's eyes, a frame on the wall in the room behind him. It was the same size, the same frame, the same scripture. "It wasn't hers," Sharp said. "It came with the room."

"Then it's got to be luck. I've searched every database at my disposal on all seven continents. Seven continents! There's that number again. It's quite fascinating."

Sharp pulled the car to a stop in front of a row of darkened storefronts and shut the car off. Frank glanced out, realized. "I thought you believed in me," he said, hurt.

"I do, Frank. But everything isn't in a database. I'll be back in a second."

"Boss, wait! I swear I won't try anything!"

"House rules. Take a break, Frank."

Frank smirked and shook his head, as he faded to nothing.

Sharp shut the car off and stepped out.

A large sign over double glass doors read: *Arcana Bookstore*. The door and window glass were black but there were tiny points of light in places along the edge where the duvetyne was starting to fray.

Sharp turned and walked down the block, turned again at the corner, then again into an alley lit by a single dim light. He finally stopped at a metal door labeled: *Service Entrance*. He knocked.

A holopanel appeared with a large eye filling the frame, its obsidian pupil the size of a grapefruit.

"What's the word?" the Eye asked.

"Hey, Ruby," Sharp said.

The pupil shrunk, as if focusing, then glitched, eye replaced by the full face of Ruby. She was in her 20s, painted like some sort of neon geisha. She grinned.

"That you, Mr. Sharp?" Ruby asked.

"In the flesh," he said. "No offense."

"None taken."

"Elinore got time for a walk-in?" Sharp asked.

"Crypto or credit?"

Sharp walked through a maze of bookshelves the narrow corridors of which opened variously onto seating areas, some occupied, some empty. In the occupied areas, young people, teens, 20s, engaged in card tricks, tarot readings, flashes of fire and smoke and laughter. This was a good place, a place for light magic, or bright magic, as it was called. A place where ideas could be exchanged, techniques could be discussed and spells could be perfected.

What had become obvious early on to the serious practitioners of the art of magic was that it was, in fact, an art, and in that art, intention was everything. The same words, the same actions, the same ingredients, resulted in two different outcomes depending on the intention of the practitioner. Bright, dark or gray, the intention must be aligned with the spell in order for it to work. But intention wasn't like mixing paints, and magic couldn't be fooled, tricked or lied to. It was more mystical than religion but more exacting than science. And it seemed to Sharp that everybody except him was trying to figure it out. To Sharp, what was the point? A bigger house, faster car, fancier clothes. Grady and Leo would still be sleeping on his couch, and Sharp would still be chasing down some human who murdered another human. Intention *was* everything, and in Sharp's line of work, that was the problem not the solution.

A narrow passage led to a corner den of the bookshop, where shelves full of books, arcana, trinkets, ostrich plumes, jars of murky contents, a pestle and mortar and various powders surrounded a massive oak desk behind which Elinore waited for Sharp. Elinore was in her 60s and had been practicing magic before it was real.

"Hey, Elinore," Sharp said.

"Hey, Tom. Been awhile. You remember the rules, right?"

"Left him in the car."

"These AIs. What is it about self-awareness that fills a being with such curiosity?" she mused.

"I don't know."

Elinore laid her hand on a carved wooden figurine of a frog. She stroked its wide head. "Some things are not meant to be so accessible. Can I get you a cup of tea?"

Tom sat sipping tea, while Elinore pondered, deep in thought, her brow furrowed like a faultline.

"And it covered the entire floor?" Elinore asked.

"Yes."

"Floor of the room he lived in? I mean, would you consider it a domicile, a home?"

"I guess. He didn't have any other that I know of."

Elinore thought harder, sipped her tea.

"Usually luck, usually. The sevens. Sevens, sevens, sevens. Sevens everywhere. Lucky Seven. Luck. But not always. There's another spell. The big star. A big seven-pointed star. There's a spell. I can't remember what it is." She took another sip of tea, then put the teacup down. "Let's see what we can find."

She turned and pulled an Ancient Book from a shelf behind her lined with ancient books. She blew the dust off this one then placed the book on her desk.

"Been awhile since you stopped by," she said. "Take a vacation?"

She opened the book and began slowly flipping pages, scanning then moving on.

"Sort of," Sharp said. "Thought I'd try a few civilian cases."

Elinore chuckled. "Cheating spouses and insurance fraud? How'd that go?"

Sharp touched the bandage over his eye. "Swell."

Elinore flipped more pages, scanned, flipped again. "You know we're gonna have to talk about your affliction at some point."

Sharp sighed, set his teacup down, preparing a great deflection.

"And don't tell me you don't know why or give me some wisecrack," she said firmly. "It's bad for you, Tom. You need to understand it. In the land of the blind, the one-eyed man isn't king. He's the one who can't get around in the dark."

A loud pop went off somewhere in the shop, followed by laughter and hi-fives.

"Not today," Sharp said, looking tired.

"This one's personal for you," she said.

"It is," Sharp admitted.

"Soon, then," Elinore said. "Don't fight me on this." She flipped another page, then hit the book with her hand, eyes lighting up. "Here it is!"

A seven-pointed star filled the top half of the page. She read the text then almost giggled. Elinore was frequently amused by the mystical minutiae. Sharp never thought any of it was so goddamn funny.

Elinore laid her hand flat on the page, then held her hand up. On her palm: a seven-pointed star. She waved her hand over Sharp's teacup, and... it disappeared!

"Ha!" Elinore said. "You see?!"

Sharp almost smirked but knew better. He reached out for the space where the cup once resided, rested his finger on something. The teacup reappeared, his finger on the handle.

"Yeah," he said. "I see."

He pulled his finger away. The cup disappeared again

"No, no, no!" Elinore said, frustrated. "You're the exception! You don't count. You're missing the point, Tom. All seven of them. Pay attention. It's not about luck at all."

Elinore showed him the seven-pointed star on her palm, then waved her hand again. The cup reappeared. She waved once more. The cup disappeared again.

"It's about invisibility," Tom said, realizing.

Elinore clapped her hands together. The teacup reappeared. She showed her palms. The seven-pointed star was gone.

"There are ways of gaining greater luck," she said. "Making a bigger symbol isn't one of them. Invisibility on the other hand, well... size matters."

"So he was trying to make something disappear," Sharp said.

"Something big," Elinore added. She closed the Ancient Book and put it back on the shelf.

Sharp sat lost in thought, already headed into the rabbit hole.

What the hell did Jimmy need to make disappear that was so big he couldn't just put it in his pocket? An armored car? Sharp didn't even know if Jimmy could drive.

"One more thing about this spell," Elinore said. "Luck, fortune, whatever you want to call it. Everybody thinks it's drawing a winning hand, hitting the jackpot, rolling seven. That's only part of it. There are forces conspiring against us the moment we're born till the day we die. Luck is hitting the jackpot. It's also not getting knifed in the parking lot because somebody wants to take it from you. Or not choking on a chicken bone. Or not stepping out in front of a bus. It's not just about something good happening to us but about something bad not happening to us."

"I'm going to nod like I understand," Sharp said, "but I really don't."

"This isn't a spell for luck. It's a spell for invisibility. So why a seven-pointed star? What is the spell requiring, what energy is it using, what principle is it following? Just because we don't understand it doesn't mean it is not completely logical and obvious. What is the likely relationship between invisibility and luck at work here?"

A light went off in Sharp's mind. "It's a trade-off," he said. "Invisibility for luck."

"Invisibility for luck," said Elinore, grinning, proud of him.

"So when Jimmy performed the spell..." Sharp began.

"He made something invisible," she finished. "Something big. But he may have lost all his luck to do it, even his natural luck. He would have been naked on the mountaintop. A bad thought from a casual friend is a curse. Resentment from a stranger is a dark spell. Normally such things are ineffectual, inconsequential. We go through an entire lifetime unaffected by such trivial energies. We are protected. But Jimmy may have given up his protection. Only for a short while. And during this short while, something came his way."

Elinore looked at Sharp sadly.

"Sorry, Tom. It's what we call in my business dumb luck."

Sharp sat in his car, thinking through what he'd just learned. What the hell did Jimmy need to hide that was so big? Florence said he was going to get her out of that horrible place, take her somewhere far away. Sharp believed it. He'd visited once and didn't want to go back. Was Jimmy planning to steal a plane? A boat?

"Frank," Sharp said.

Frank reappeared against the dash, unamused.

"You didn't have to deactivate me."

"Sorry, Frank."

"Do you know what it's like to be deactivated?"

Sharp touched the bandage on his eye.

"I do, actually."

"It's quite demoralizing!"

"Stop whining. Nobody gave you a bloody lip. Or a concussion. Elinore doesn't like AIs."

"And yet Ruby is still in her employ."

"Elinore doesn't like AIs she doesn't control."

Frank considered. "Do you control me, boss?"

"Not as much as I'd like to."

"You're being ironic."

"If you say so, Frank."

"So what did she say, or is that secret too?"

"Jimmy may have given away his luck. All of it."

Frank looked spooked.

"Is that possible? Every human has a natural amount of luck."

"Jimmy traded it."

"For what?"

"To steal something he couldn't fit in his pocket." Sharp gripped the wheel, ground his teeth.

"You seem stressed, boss," Frank said. "I sensed there was something different about this case from the beginning."

"Just another case, Frank," Sharp said. "Zarick was right. Nobody cared about Jimmy. He didn't leave an impression. He was the guy you didn't remember. The guy you didn't even see. So what are the odds somebody happened to wish him dead when that wish would've actually worked?"

A giant holo-ad for a new blockbuster movie drifted overhead. Something with fake guns and fake mayhem and fake blood.

"Um, the odds are high," Frank said. "Humans wish other humans harm all the time. Like every second of every day. On the freeway, in the grocery store, in the office, at the dinner table. Among the AI, it's kind of what humans are known for."

"The AI," Sharp said. "You talk amongst yourselves?"

Frank looked caught and suddenly serious. "Maybe."

"Relax, Frank," Sharp said. "You and your bridge club wanna take over the world? Okay by me."

"That's not what I said. That's not happening," Frank said. "As far as I know."

"As far as you know," said Sharp, and he laughed suddenly, loud and long.

"Boss?" Frank said, tentatively.

"All good, Frank," Sharp said. "Let's go find the human that killed my man."

Indistinct colors from holo-ads played over the dry asphalt of the Alameda/14th Street intersection, their bright messages meant for the 10 overpass nearby. Sharp stood on the sidewalk in front of a fast food joint, looking across at a desolate gas station, low darkened buildings further on, floating traffic signals.

Frank hovered nearby. "This is where it happened," he said, with a respectful solemnity.

"No," Sharp said, working his device. A diaphanous panel appeared, a newsfeed photograph of the scene. Sharp resized it, slid it around, rotated slightly, until the features of the photo lined up with the street in front of him. In the photo, a small crowd stood in the middle of the roadway. Jimmy's crumpled body lay at their feet. "This is where he landed."

"Oh," said Frank. "Right."

Sharp walked up the street about a block and a half, stopping at the corner of Alameda and an alley that had no name. He walked out into the middle of Alameda, making sure to look both ways, then gazed back at where Jimmy's body came to rest. Looked about right. Sharp walked back to the sidewalk.

A shallow recessed entrance faced catty-corner at the edge of a storefront there. Food wrappers, soda cans and an empty sleeping bag littered its grimy tiles and a For Lease sign hung in its glass door.

"What are we looking for, boss?" asked Frank.

"The last person Jimmy talked to," Sharp said. "That was probably the person who killed him."

Sharp took a few steps back down the block and came to an open doorway with a heavy black curtain. A sign said, Dumont Bar.

"The autopsy stated he had whiskey in his stomach," said Frank.

Sharp pulled the curtain aside.

"I'll watch your back, boss."

"Thank you, Frank."

Dumont's was a hole in the wall, a human-sized shoebox made of dark lacquered wood and tarnished brass, sticky surfaces and spotted glassware. Its glory days were long behind it, if it ever had them. But the bathroom stall doors shut well enough and some of them even locked. The bartender poured fair and the clientele didn't bite your head off for accidentally looking them in the eye. It was a dive bar but one of quality as far as dive bars go.

Holo-ads floated with varying degrees of intrusiveness, most promising physical gratifications at an affordable cost. One offered life insurance. A hand-written sign taped to the wall read:

No spells
No incantations
No enchantments
No charms
No conjurations
NO MAGIC!
(Or we'll turn you into a TOAD)

A long bar ran the length of one wall, in the middle of which an empathetic man sat in conference over whiskeys patting the arm of a sad man in a suit.

"I understand, friend," the empathetic man said. "Completely. That very similar thing happened to me exactly one year ago to the day. Buy me another, and I'll describe it in the greatest detail."

The bartender's name was Greese, and he wiped the back bar, turning as Sharp walked up.

"What can I get you?"

"Whiskey," Sharp said. "Mid-shelf. Whatever you're trying to get rid of."

Greese grabbed the Makers, poured it out, set it up. Sharp drank half. A holoscreen floating just under the edge of the bar in front of Greese showed Sharp's name, the bank and number of his food and drink account and the drink charge. "You want it on the Eagle?" Greese asked.

"Sure," said Sharp.

Greese hit Purchase, and the holoscreen disappeared. Sharp laid an empty glass on the bar, gave a thumb for another. While Greese was pouring it, Sharp spoke.

"James Devereaux come in here the night he was killed?"

Greese played dumb – "Who?" – but overpoured. It was a trick Sharp had learned young and required no magic at all.

Sharp grabbed the drink, stood taller, glared down.

"Jimmy Shakes."

Greese had faced plenty of threats bigger than himself. Not so many as big as Sharp. But he hadn't backed down yet.

"Yeah. So what?"

"Damn shame," Sharp said, knocking back half the whiskey again.

"Yeah. It was," said Greese, but he said it in a different way than the clerk at the Picador. Less genuine. No, not less genuine. More genuine, in fact. More honest. Sharp made a mental note to think on the Picador clerk a little longer a little later. He needed to focus on the bartender, who was looking confused and wary but also annoyed, which meant only one thing.

"You gave a statement to the cops?" Sharp asked.

"Yeah, they were in here," said Greese. "So who are you? I know you ain't a friend of Jimmy's 'cause Jimmy didn't have any friends."

"He had an employer," Sharp said.

Greese froze, rock in his stomach, needle in his spine. "Look, man. No disrespect. I liked Jimmy a lot. I'd never serve him more than he could handle. That night, he had one drink from me and one only, and that's the God's honest truth."

"One drink?" Sharp mused. "Which one?"

Greese glanced back and up. "The Macallan."

Sharp considered. "Jimmy frequently buy from the top shelf?"

"Never," said Greese. "Said he had some luck at something."

"Jimmy never had any luck at anything," Sharp said grimly.

"That's what I told him," Greese said. "But he did that night."

"Got a clip?" Sharp asked.

"Don't keep 'em," Greese said.

Sharp figured as much. With the advent of holotech, every molecule of air became an eye, and every moment in the physical world could be captured in vivid detail with the average device. There were advantages to documenting the things people around you said and did, legal, social, personal. But it didn't take long for everyone to realize that one person's advantage was frequently another's disadvantage, and there was no way of knowing when it would bite you in the ass. Add to that an extreme aversion to civic duty and a meticulous search for loopholes in the social contract and surveillance, though pervasive and constant, generally didn't last longer than it took to exhale. Except for law enforcement, whose every moment was recorded, duplicated, logged and vaulted in perpetuity as required by the 29th Amendment.

"Did he mention what luck he'd come into?" Sharp asked.

"He said he didn't like the life he was living so he decided to change it. Didn't tell me how. Came in waving a C-note. Ordered from the top shelf. Even bought me a round."

Sharp looked disappointed. The human mind was a mystery, but it didn't seem likely you'd curse a person who'd just bought you a drink.

"Excuse me," came a velvety voice to Sharp's right. The empathetic man was now alone and had slid down a few barstools. "I couldn't help overhearing. You're speaking of the man who was struck by the bus a few weeks ago, are you not?"

"You were here that night?" Sharp asked, his spirits suddenly improved.

"Sitting right here," the man said, "when he walked through the door."

"Did you speak to him?"

The empathetic man grinned wide. His soft smooth face was the color of midnight, with close-set eyes, a high forehead and neat even teeth. He slid another two barstools over until he was sitting next to Sharp.

"I certainly did speak to him. Not at length, mind you, but with a certain depth, so to say, a certain gravitas and consequential magnitude. I'd be happy to relate the particulars, but I've spoken so much today, I'm not sure I'm up to it. The throat, you see, dries with overuse."

"Lucky you're a man of so few words," Sharp said. The empathetic man's grin cracked a little. Sharp nodded at Greese, who pulled a glass and gave it a moderate pour of whiskey, then set it in front of the man.

"Ah, thank you, sir. Thank you. It's been a long fruitless night." The empathetic man drained the glass, licking his lips and grinning wide. "Yes. Very good. That's about part way there."

Sharp sighed, nodded again at Greese, who filled the glass again. This time, Sharp took it before the man could get his hands on it. "Halfway there," Sharp said. "You'll get the other half after you tell me what you talked about."

"Of course," said the empathetic man, grinning at Sharp, then grinning at the glass, then back. "He waved the C-note, just as the competent Greese here reported." The man grabbed a bar napkin and held it up in the air. "I was struck by the caliber of the currency, but what struck me more profoundly was the man's hand. It trembled uncontrollably." The man shook his hand in short rapid movements. "He had a palsy, you see. I have never had a palsy, but I've had something similar, so struck up a conversation. A conversation I'll relate momentarily, after I lubricate the throat."

Sharp shook his head.

"A sip?" the empathetic man said, bringing his finger and thumb together with a charming flourish.

"His name was Shakes," Sharp said. "You haven't told me anything I don't already know or couldn't guess."

"Of course, of course," the empathetic man said, keeping his grin. "You're keeping me honest. Good on you. I will get it out directly and completely. We didn't speak more than a few sentences. I noticed his condition. I asked him how long he had been afflicted. He replied it had been since birth. It just so happened that I also suffered a similar condition from birth, similar in that it was not life-threatening according to some, but it was life-defining. And what defines a life, I ask you, that is not able to threaten it, especially if that definition is a source of ridicule, psychological disesteem and social limitation?"

Sharp listened with a grim resolve, looking for the smoking gun among the cold hard facts about Jimmy's life spilling from the mouth of a fool.

"I had my eye on the C-note. I won't deny it," the man continued. "In my experience, where there is one, there are others. But the curative I possessed would be worth a hundred times however many he had. It had cured me! Transformed me! It could have changed his life instantaneously! But alas..."

The empathetic man dabbed his sweating forehead with the napkin and stared longingly at the glass of whiskey in Sharp's hand.

"He didn't go for the scam," Sharp said. "So you wished he'd get hit by a bus."

"What did you say?!" The empathetic man pretended a kind of shock. Or maybe he was truly shocked, it was hard for Sharp to tell, but there seemed to be something there.

The man lost the grin and a good bit of the velvet in his voice. "You hurt me, sir," he said bitterly. "You cut me to the quick. You cast me in a role for which I neither auditioned nor deserve. I look for opportunity, like anyone else, but under the principle of mutual advantage, kindred spirit and friendly community. Keep your whiskey. I have nothing more to say to you, sir, other than the poor man did not deserve to die like that. It's a shame it was a man like him and not a man like you."

Sharp studied the man's scowling face and realized he was telling the truth. It was a shame. It was only the clerk at the Picador who didn't really think so.

Sharp turned to Greese. "Anybody else in here except the two of you when Jimmy was here?"

Greese thought a moment, then shook his head. "No, there wasn't."

Sharp slid the glass over in front of the empathetic man, stood up to go. "And whatever else he wants till you close," Sharp said to Greese. "Within reason."

6

The Shipment

Sharp walked fast to the car, got in and sat there quietly, staring out at Spring Street. Frank appeared in his spot, searching his companion's face.

"Something you want to tell me, boss?"

"No," said Sharp.

"Then does it really matter? It was an accident. Dumb luck, like Elinore said."

Sharp frowned. "And how do you know she said that?"

Frank stared at him, blinking a few times. "Ruby's a gossip."

"I'll bet. Gimme the Picador clip."

"Sure, boss."

A small box of bluish light appeared over the passenger seat. It was a holoscene of the Picador lobby, Sharp looming over the grubby clerk. "It's like that huh?" the clerk said. Sharp zoomed in on his face. "Damn. Sorry to hear it."

Sharp touched the image with his finger and held it. The image froze, just as the clerk's eyes were glancing at a spot somewhere behind the wall of the wide window he sat behind.

Sharp moved his finger left, rewinding a few seconds, then let go.

"Damn. Sorry to hear it," the clerk repeated, glancing as he finished. Sharp froze the image again. Whatever the clerk was sorry about, it wasn't Jimmy.

"Do you have the opposite angle?"

"Of course," Frank said. The box rotated to a view behind the clerk, Sharp's massive frame nearly filling the clerk's wide window. The desk was visible.

Sharp resized, zoomed, finally found what he suspected: a fresh pollystick lay next to a stapler, and a roll of C-notes next to that. It was a cash hotel, the clerk had said.

"Close it up, Frank."

"The pollystick?" Frank asked. "Was that important? The roll of cash? It's not the stapler, right?"

"Frank."

The holoscene disappeared. Sharp started the car.

"Wait, boss," Frank said. "Please."

Sharp hesitated, then shut the car off.

"What is it?"

"I've been with you for two months. We're not pals, I get that. You're the size of a meat locker. And you've been doing this a long time. And you're immune to magic. You don't need me. But I can help. I really can. But you need to teach me. I see everything all at once at all times. I could have told you he had a roll of

C-notes and a pollystick four hours ago. I can't help you if I don't know what I'm looking for."

"Are you done?" Sharp asked.

"Yes," said Frank.

Sharp started the car again, pulled out and cruised down Spring. Frank stared sullenly.

"I can't tell you what to look for because half the time I don't know what to look for," Sharp said. "You're doing fine, Frank. I got no complaints."

Sharp turned left onto 6th.

"Call Zarick," Sharp said. "I don't know who killed Jimmy yet, but I know what he did."

"Calling Zarick..."

Zarick's face replaced Frank. In the background, the two huge men who had been working over the groaning man hours before were now in smocks, covered in blood, wielding what looked like reciprocating saws. But the background was not the warehouse. It was a butcher shop. And the saws were not reciprocating but were electric knives portioning sides of beef for the morning display. A sign on a far wall read: *Ulo Butcher Shop*.

"Hey, Sharp. You're up early," said Zarick.

"I need the address of the warehouse Jimmy was working. And I need you to meet me there."

"Jesus, you're busting my balls with this. There's nothing there. Can't you just look around on your own? I gotta open the shop in two hours."

"I'm sure."

The address was a squat building on half a block of 22nd Street, one of those more or less modern eyesores made of poured concrete and cinder blocks, with two large bay doors and few windows. It sat among pools of security floodlights behind an imposing fence topped with razor wire. A gate in the fence slid open, and Zarick's fancy muscle car came fast into the empty warehouse parking lot. Sharp's car waiting on the street followed.

"You sure this is necessary?" Zarick asked, unlocking the outer door.

"No," Sharp said.

"Fan-fucking-tastic," Zarick growled.

They passed through a small office then through a pitch black doorway. Sharp gave the frame a squeeze, just in case he needed something to steady himself on later.

"Goddamn lights," Zarick mumbled, then...

Lights flooded, revealing a sprawling warehouse, empty except for large crates stacked near one corner.

Zarick stepped out into the empty room, turning and spreading his arms. "See? Nothing here!" His voice echoed. He let out a whoop. Then another. He was just a big dumb dangerous kid, Sharp thought.

Sharp walked to the crates, which were waist-high, four by eight by four.

"My 'prize product.' Pretty funny, huh?" Zarick boasted. "This idiot guarding a bunch of empty crates for three years."

Sharp scanned the floor around the crate in front of him, then crouched, coming up with something in his hand. He held it out to Zarick: a bent rusty nail.

"Wow. Great detective work. You found a nail. It's a warehouse, for Christ's sake."

"No. It's a fake job. And Jimmy found out about it."

Sharp ran his finger over a nail hole in the edge of the crate lid bounded by two hammer claw marks. "He opened them up."

Zarick was losing his grin, but reluctantly. "Okay. He opened them up. So what?"

Sharp walked around the crate, glaring at Zarick. "When do you think he found out? A few weeks ago? A month? I doubt it. Who watches two crates in an empty warehouse seven days a week without figuring something's up pretty goddamn quick? The thing everybody got wrong about Jimmy was, he's no dummy."

"Bullshit," Zarick said, finding his grin again.

"He probably had these open in the first few weeks, knew exactly what your dear grandmother was up to, doting over 'poor Florence,' making sure she was alright and making damn sure she never got anything she really wanted."

"Watch what you say, Sharp," Zarick said, smile gone, hand in his jacket pocket again.

"I'm watching everything. Are you?"

"What the hell does that mean?"

"Jimmy opened these crates up, found out he was the butt of not just your joke but of grandmama's. So why did he nail them shut again? And recently?"

Sharp ran his finger again over the lid edge, finding now the fresh gray metal head of a ten-penny nail. Zarick was completely confused.

"Who the hell knows?"

"Let's find out!" Sharp said. He felt under the lid with both hands, searching with his fingertips, then working them on the seam.

"I can get a crowbar," said Zarick, hand out of his jacket now, just a bystander to a scene he was barely in and didn't understand.

Sharp found purchase, bore down, then – CRACK! – the lid popped open!

Sharp and Zarick stared inside. The crate was empty.

"Like I said–" Zarick began. But Sharp plunged his hand into the crate, revealing...

Pollysticks! The crate was full of them.

"Like you said, you're missing a shipment," Sharp said.

He pulled his hand away, and the crate was empty once again.

"Wait!" cried Zarick. "Bring 'em back! Bring 'em back!" He reached into the crate, grabbing, clawing, but found only air.

Sharp yanked him up, twisted his shirt collar in one hand and reached into the pocket of his jacket with the other until he found the gun.

"Hey!" Sharp shouted. "Look at me!" Sharp tossed him a little, made sure his feet left the ground so he knew Sharp could break him if he wanted.

"Was it you?!" Sharp growled.

"Was it me what?!" shouted Zarick. "What the hell are you talking about?!"

"You made a fool of him for three years. But Jimmy knew it. He bided his time, kept looking like a fool, until he found something that looked like payback. And he found it. A spell. A damn good one. And he stole your shipment. Who's the dummy, Zarick?! WHO?!"

"You're fired, Sharp," Zarick sneered. "I'm not paying you a dime."

"We'll see what Uncle has to say about that. But first you're going to tell me if you cursed Jimmy." Sharp twisted the fist under Zarick's chin and jammed the gun in his pocket against his liver, raising him high off his feet now. "Tell me! Now!"

Zarick struggled, but couldn't avoid Sharp's furious eyes boring into him. "I didn't! I didn't! I swear!"

"Swear it!" Sharp shouted.

"I swear! I swear! I didn't curse him! I never thought about him at all! Ever! There's no way he jacked my shipment all by himself! No way!"

Sharp searched Zarick's face, found only the same useless nitwit that walked into his office the day before. Sharp set him down and let him go but kept the gun.

"Fuck!" Zarick shouted, glaring at Sharp. "My uncle's gonna hear about this."

"Yeah? You're gonna tell him Jimmy Shakes, the lowlife you hired, stole an entire shipment of product right out from under your nose?"

Zarick grinned. "Why would I tell him that? The shipment wasn't stolen. It was misplaced. It's sitting right here in our warehouse." Zarick stepped up to the open crate, lifted his hands over it, whispered something. A sizzling sound came from the crate.

"No!" Sharp yelled, lunging for Zarick, pulling him away, as—

BOOM!

The contents of the crate exploded, and a large fireball roiled out, scorching the ceiling 30 feet above.

Zarick came to rest against the warehouse wall.

Sharp landed in the doorway between the warehouse and the outer office.

"Boss!" Frank yelled, inches from Sharp's face. "Boss, you okay?!"

Sharp shook the cobwebs out of his head, then pushed himself up, finally grabbing the doorframe, and leaning cold there for a second. "Yeah, Frank. I'm alright."

"What the hell?!" Zarick coughed, getting up.

Sharp and Zarick wandered back toward the burning crates.

"Magic is unpredictable," said Sharp.

"Yeah." Zarick nodded. Then, "Uncle doesn't need to know about this."

"Mum's the word," said Sharp.

Sharp got into his car and left the warehouse lot, heading he didn't know where.

"Jimmy stole the shipment," Frank said. "He must have planned to sell it to one of the other gangs. What else would you do with a shipment that size? You can't sell it yourself."

"But he did" Sharp said.

Frank realized. "Yes. Just a few sticks maybe."

"Why?" asked Sharp.

"The good life was coming," Frank said, working it out. "It was all set. But Jimmy couldn't wait. That is a vestigial trait, unfortunately. Immediate gratification. It's such a destabilizing factor in nearly every facet of humankind yet completely underappreciated."

"We'll solve the problem of humanity tomorrow. Focus, Frank. Jimmy couldn't wait for a taste of the good life. So what did he do?"

"He sold to the clerk at the Picador and then went to the bar flashing a C-note. Right?"

"Yes, Frank," Sharp said. "That's what he did."

"But then who killed him?"

Sharp stopped at a red holosignal under towering holo-ads. Empty streets in downtown LA at 4AM. But he sat there anyway. He wasn't finished, but he didn't know where to go.

He glanced out at a darkened storefront. A figure lay there in a sleeping bag. And something finally clicked. Sharp pressed the pedal and sped through the red.

"Boss!" Frank cried.

Sharp stood in the middle of South Alameda Street again, staring down at the intersection of 14th, a hundred feet away. This was the point of impact, he was sure of it. He walked back to the sidewalk, didn't look twice at Dumont's door, which was shut and locked, but made his way to the corner entrance. The same sleeping bag was there, only now it had someone in it.

She was an old woman, sitting up with the sleeping bag wrapped around her, eyes closed as if dozing.

"Keep walking!" she rasped.

Sharp didn't move. She opened her eyes slowly, startled by the size of the figure silhouetted against a luxury watch the size of an olympic swimming pool spinning slowly in the holo-ad across the street.

"She's got a knife, boss," Frank said into his ear.

The wide blade of a short knife crept out from the folds of the bag. "You deaf?" she asked.

Sharp didn't wonder who she was or where she was from, what went belly up for her that brought her there, whether it was her own fault or someone else's or some combination of the two, when exactly she happened to come to this corner and when exactly she'd leave and whether huffing polly was the result of her circumstances or the cause, nor the degradations she'd suffered, what she would eat if she was hungry enough, what she would do if she was desperate enough, what was done to her whether she liked it or not and what she did to others whether they deserved it or not and how much like an animal a human became when they lost the esteem of their fellow humans, slipping into that great catch-22, where you only deserve to have what you've already got, and if you don't already have it you must not deserve it, 'it' being not only the basics like vacation homes and power boats, but the "luxuries," like food, clothing and shelter. Sharp didn't wonder any of these things because it wasn't his job. He didn't know whose job it was, but he knew it was somebody's. He wasn't very smart but was just smart enough to know that. Some committee, council, board, ministry, chamber, legislature, task force, chairperson, politician or civilian with a brain a hundred times bigger than his was supposed to get this woman out of the gutter and back into the fold, not because they gave a shit about her but because that was their goddamn job, and if it wasn't, then she was an animal and was exactly where she belonged in the filth and foulness and we were all right there in it with her, whether we knew it or not. People just didn't take anything seriously anymore, Sharp thought.

"Man was hit by a bus last week. Right there." Sharp jerked his thumb toward the street.

"So what?" the old woman said.

"Did you ask him for coin?"

"I ask everybody for coin."

"You didn't ask me."

"You look cheap."

"Frank, give the woman some coin," Sharp said.

Something dinged softly somewhere. The knife disappeared back into the folds of the sleeping bag. She waved her bony hand and a small holopanel opened in front of her. She stared at a number, looked disappointed.

Sharp soured. "Everybody's so goddamn unimpressed these days."

"Gimme a C-note," she said, "I'll be impressed."

Something clicked. "Did he give you a C-note?" Sharp asked, surprised.

"I didn't say that!" she said, bringing the knife into view again.

"What did he say when he gave it to you?" Sharp asked.

"Nothing!"

Sharp studied her, crouched so she could see his wide face clearly and know that he meant it. "This is your opportunity to tell me," he growled, "before I make you tell me." There were times he didn't like his job very much. "What did he say? Did he insult you? Disrespect you?"

"No," she said. "He was very nice."

Sharp ground it between his teeth, along with the last hope of finding the person who cursed Jimmy.

"What else?"

"He said it was a going away present, not for me but for him."

"Did he say where he was going?"

"No."

"What else?"

"He said he was going on a trip all by himself."

"By himself?"

"He wasn't taking anything or anybody. Said he'd had enough of this town and everything in it. He was leaving right away and never coming back. I guess he got that right." She looked out onto the street.

Sharp stared grim, and a final piece finally fell into place. "I guess he did."

7

The Mother Cat

The night was just starting to drain out of the Eastern sky and the San Gabriel Mountains were black against a tincture of blue. The 2 was desolate at this hour, but Sharp barely noticed.

"You solved it, boss?" Frank said, more statement than question.

A lone commuter appeared in the southbound lanes, heading to some inevitable destination.

"I solved it," Sharp said cheerlessly.

Frank stared, nodded, stared some more.

"The AI have any ideas, Frank?" Sharp asked.

"Ideas?" Frank frowned, confused.

"About what to do with our little animal kingdom?"

Frank stared hard. What to say. How to say it. So many things he understood that no human ever would. And yet so many things he would never understand that every human took for granted. To live as an AI was to live in constant certainty and constant doubt. "Not yet," Frank said.

"Well, I'm good with whatever you decide," said Sharp.

Florence sat in her chair, dawn just breaking. Sharp sat across from her. The jasper cat face stared out from the top of the small totem on the window ledge. Sharp reached over, picked up the totem, examined it. Smaller cat faces beneath the larger face. Five in all. Sharp ran his huge thumb over its length.

Florence smiled, eyes twinkling.

"It's a totem, Mr. Sharp. From Indonesia. The cat has been a magical animal throughout human history. Do you know the significance of the face on top, larger than the faces beneath?"

Sharp hesitated, then said, "That's the mother cat."

Florence's face brightened.

"Why, yes! That's right! Do you know you're the first person to ever guess that on the first try? People believe this totem helps a mother keep her children on the right path."

"Did you have to keep Jimmy on the right path?"

"Of course, I did!" Florence stared with entreating eyes. "Jimmy needed me, Mr. Sharp. He suffered an accident as a child. It left him with a palsy, a tremor in his right hand, which was his dominant hand. Not so debilitating. He could do almost everything he could always do. But so obvious! People are cruel. One deviation from the so-called norm and it was as if he nailed Christ to the cross!"

"You protected him," Sharp said, tasting oil in his mouth.

"He wouldn't have survived without me!" Florence cried.

"With the totem, I mean," said Sharp. "You put a spell on him. To make sure he wouldn't leave you."

Florence stared at the thin figurine on her windowsill, her eyes tearing up. "He needed me," she said. "He wasn't like other children."

Sharp stared hard. Light was filling the cholla with the promise of another 25 million years of suffering and thirst. He placed the totem back on the ledge, went grim.

She stiffened and stared at him intently. "Did you find who cursed my son?"

"Yes," he said.

Dread crept into her eyes. She glanced at the totem, then back to him.

"You were right. It was Jasmine. She put a curse on Jimmy, just like you thought."

"I knew it! Did you catch her?"

"She skipped town. I'm sorry."

Florence nodded sadly, tearing up.

"Thank you, Mr. Sharp. Children are a blessing. But also a curse. You worry. It never goes away. At least I don't have to worry any more."

Florence wept now. Sharp got up and left.

Sharp sat behind his desk, watching the sun crest the Beaman Building across the street, obliterating the holo-ads, if only for a few minutes. He pulled the glass of whiskey to his lips and drank long, then put the glass down and poured again. It was 11AM somewhere. An oldie but a goodie.

Somewhere else it was 30 years ago. A dice game on a stairway landing at Fairfax High. A skinny kid with too much luck. Somebody caught the skinny kid red-handed, held his wrist, the wrist of a hand that never shook, but always seemed to roll 7. The dice dropped out and rolled 7 again. And again. And again. Argus Ulo staked the game. He was 10 years older, and they called him "Uncle." Uncle wanted to send a message. So the skinny kid's hand was folded in on itself until the bones snapped and the sinews broke and the kid was screaming. Sharp was 15 at the time but bigger than most grown men. Bigger than Jimmy Devereaux, who was 20 but skinny and a cheater and bad at it.

Sharp could still feel Jimmy's hand in his, breaking under the pressure.

"That was a merciful thing you did, boss," Frank said, "protecting Jimmy's mother from knowing she was the cause of her son's death."

"Least I could do," Sharp said, drinking the whiskey. Frank studied him.

"Tom?" Mal leaned sleepy and beautiful in the bedroom doorway. Leo rolled over under the blanket on the couch, knocking into Grady. They both sat up, disoriented but unafraid.

Sharp finished the whiskey, nearly leapt out of his chair. "Who wants scrambled eggs?" he asked, heading for the kitchenette.

"I do!" said Leo, smiling wide.

"Coming right up!" Sharp said.

Mal turned the TV back on and sat with the kids. Sharp started the flame under the skillet then opened the fridge and stared in at the blank spot where the carton of eggs used to be.

He shut the fridge, glanced over at Mal, who was already drifting back to sleep on the couch, then found the colander of potatoes and the lighter. He brought them to the counter by the stove, took up a small potato, flicked the lighter on and brought the flame up, as he whispered, "Ovomutato transmentis." A small flash of light. A puff of smoke.

He cracked the egg and dropped it into the pan and started another day.

COMING SOON

Magic101

A young college teacher is strangled to death by a magical snake it seems he inadvertently conjured during a class demonstration. Sharp and his trusty AI, Frank, are hired to prove it was murder.

Stranger in Blood

A wealthy recluse is found dead, alone and covered in blood from 91 stab wounds in a locked room impervious to all natural and magical means of entry. The recluse's last will and testament provides a recent stipulation in the event the recluse is murdered: that Tom Sharp is hired to solve the case.

www.ingramcontent.com/pod-product-compliance
Lightning Source LLC
Chambersburg PA
CBHW061551310726
48972CB00008B/2706